F
HAY

Haywood, Carolyn.

Eddie's friend
Boodles.

$12.95

33197000026281

DATE			
T			

DISCARDED

Eddie's Friend
BOODLES

Carolyn Haywood

PICTURES BY
CATHERINE STOCK

Morrow Junior Books
New York

Text copyright © 1991 by Carolyn Haywood
Illustrations copyright © 1991 by Catherine Stock
All rights reserved.
No part of this book may be reproduced or utilized
in any form or by any means,
electronic or mechanical,
including photocopying, recording or by any
information storage and retrieval system,
without permission in writing from the Publisher.
Inquiries should be addressed to
William Morrow and Company, Inc.,
1350 Avenue of the Americas,
New York, N.Y. 10019.
Printed in the United States of America.
1 2 3 4 5 6 7 8 9 10
Library of Congress Cataloging-in-Publication Data
Haywood, Carolyn, 1898–1990
Eddie's friend Boodles / Carolyn Haywood ; illustrations by
Catherine Stock.
p.   cm.
Summary: A visit to the circus inspires Boodles to experiment with
clown makeup and to try to teach his dog Poochie to do tricks.
ISBN 0-688-09028-1
[1. Circus—Fiction. 2. Dogs—Fiction. 3. Humorous stories.]
I. Stock, Catherine, ill. II. Title.
PZ7.H31496Eead 1991
[Fic]—dc20 91-3212 CIP AC

This book is lovingly dedicated to
Eric Cameron Bachmann
C. H.

Contents

·1·

Funzies Are Fun!

One autumn afternoon, Eddie Wilson and his best friend, Boodles, jumped out of the school bus at the corner. They were on their way to Boodles's house.

"Did I ever tell you," said Boodles, "about my Uncle Sam Walker? He was the most famous circus clown the world has ever known."

"No," said Eddie. "You never told me that. When the circus comes to town, will

1

your Uncle Sam be in it?"

"Of course not," replied Boodles. "He's retired."

Boodles's real name was Boswell Carey, after his great-grandfather, who had been a famous lawyer. Boswell was supposed to take after him.

One day, when Boswell was a baby, his grandmother dropped in to see him. Boswell was in his playpen. His grandmother looked down and said, "Boo!"

To her surprise, the baby grinned. He puckered up his little mouth and said, "Bco!" right back.

After that, he greeted everyone with a grin and a "Boo!" Soon the whole family was calling him Boodles. When he went to school, all the children called him Boodles. Even his teachers called him Boodles.

Now Eddie could hardly remember that Boodles had another name.

Today Eddie and Boodles were looking forward to Saturday, when the circus was coming to town. They could hardly wait to see the circus parade and then go to the show in the big tent. It was going to be a great day.

As they walked into the family room at the Careys' house, Boodles's little dog, Poochie, ran to greet them. "Funny I never told you about my Uncle Sam, who was the world's greatest clown," Boodles said to Eddie.

Boodles's brother, Hal, lifted his head from the dictionary and said, "Boodles! What do you mean? You know we don't have an uncle named Sam."

"Sure we do!" Boodles was grinning. "Sam Walker—the world's greatest clown."

Hal looked astonished. Years before, the brothers had seen Sam Walker perform. He truly was the greatest clown in the world. Boodles had hung a circus poster of the clown in his bedroom.

"Boodles," Hal said. "Sam Walker is not a relative of ours. What do you mean telling a lie like that?"

"Oh," said Boodles, "it's not a real lie. It's just a funzie."

"A funzie!" said Hal. "What is a funzie?"

"Well, it's something that I know isn't true, but I love to say it, and Eddie here, he knows it isn't true, but he likes hearing about it. You see," Boodles continued,

3

"sometimes I can't get to sleep at night, and I lie in bed and think up funzies. It's the way Eddie and I have fun."

"That's right," said Eddie. "I do it, too. I tell Boodles a lot of things that we know aren't true. It's fun."

"You two have a crazy idea of fun!" said Hal, laughing. "Just make sure you know the difference between a funzie and a lie, Boodles."

"Oh, I do," Boodles told him.

Saturday came at last. Eddie and Boodles got up early, and together they walked downtown. They found a good spot right on the curb, where they could watch the circus parade. At first the boys sat down, but before long they jumped to their feet.

"Look, Eddie," cried Boodles, "here they come!"

It was a wonderful circus parade. First came a group of police officers, leading the band down the street. Next came the elephants, passing right in front of the boys. Each elephant held on to the tail of the one in front with its trunk.

There were bareback riders in glittery costumes and acrobats who did handstands

5

and flips. Then the clowns marched by, waving and joking with the crowd. Two of them had dogs dressed in funny collars. A lot of ordinary-looking people were just walking along, and, at the very end, four strong horses were pulling two lions in a beautiful red-and-yellow cage.

"Who do you think they are, Eddie?" Boodles asked, pointing to the ordinary-looking people.

"Well, I guess they're the trapeze artists or lion tamers," said Eddie. "They haven't got their costumes on yet."

After the parade was over, the boys followed the crowd over to the fairgrounds. The big colorful circus tent was already set up, and the air smelled of cotton candy and popcorn. A great many people were milling around. Among them was a man with a big bunch of brightly colored balloons. He held a beautiful red balloon up to Boodles. Boodles took it and started walking away, but the man came running after him.

"Hey! Hey!" shouted the balloon man. When he caught up to Boodles, he tugged the string of the beautiful red balloon and said, "Say, buster, where's your dollar for this balloon?"

"Dollar?" asked Boodles. "I didn't know you were selling them. I'm sorry. I thought you were giving them away."

"Giving them away!" shouted the man. "They're a dollar each, and either you give me a dollar or give me the balloon."

Very sadly, Boodles handed over the balloon. It was such a beautiful red balloon, so shiny and big. He hated to part with it. He put his hand deep into his pocket. He felt the four quarters his mother had given him to buy peanuts for the elephants. But he couldn't resist the balloon, so he handed the quarters to the man and took it back.

Now Boodles and Eddie went to look at the elephants. Boodles was sorry he didn't have any peanuts for them, but Eddie still had some money in his pocket, and he bought a bag.

A few steps more and they were in front of one of the elephants. "Say, Eddie," said Boodles, "could you let me have a few of those peanuts to give to the elephant?"

"Sure," said Eddie. "Help yourself." He held out the bag of peanuts to Boodles. But before Boodles could take it, the elephant's trunk came over the fence and picked up the whole bag. In a minute, the peanuts had disappeared in the elephant's mouth.

"Wow, did you see that?" exclaimed Boodles.

"I think that elephant is a big pig!" said Eddie.

"You're right," said Boodles. "He's a pig, all right. I didn't know there were any pig elephants, but he's one for sure."

Now that there were no more peanuts, the boys went over to the entrance to one of the sideshows. There they found a clown, with his dog sitting beside him.

Boodles stopped beside the clown and said, "Did you ever know the famous clown Sam Walker?"

"Oh, no," said the clown. "He was too famous to know anybody so *un*famous as I, but we all admired him and thought he was wonderful."

"I did, too," said Boodles. He wanted so much to say that this famous clown, Sam Walker, was his uncle; but Boodles knew that it wasn't true. He knew he couldn't tell a funzie to this clown because this clown didn't know about funzies. So instead, Boodles said to him, "I'm going to be a clown when I grow up. I'm going to be a clown as

good as Sam Walker was. I'm going to start right away to try different kinds of makeup, and I'm going to teach my dog to do tricks."

"Well," said the clown, "I'm sure you'll make a very good clown, so have plenty of fun getting ready to join the circus."

"I will," said Boodles. "It was nice to meet you." He shook the clown's hand. "So long! We'll see you this afternoon inside the tent."

·2·

Balloons and Sandwiches

As Boodles and Eddie were leaving the circus grounds, they saw Boodles's mother waiting for them at the entrance. Both boys were glad to see that she was carrying a large picnic basket. "I've brought our lunch," she said. "And there are picnic tables back of the circus tent where we can eat. Just follow me."

Boodles's mother led the boys to the picnic area. Many people were already

11

seated at the tables. At one of them, there was a little boy with a red balloon like Boodles's. He was no more than two years old. He was pulling on the string of the balloon, making it bounce up and down over his head.

Suddenly, he let go of the string and the balloon floated away toward the sky. The little boy screamed. Everyone watched as he stretched out his arms, trying to get the balloon to come back. But the balloon went on skyward, and the little boy screamed louder and louder.

All this time, Boodles's mother was looking for a place at a table where they could sit and have lunch. Soon she found a table where only a man and a woman were seated. Boodles's mother asked whether they could use the vacant places. The man and the woman said that they would be happy to share the table.

The little boy went on screaming. His mother tried to quiet him, but the screaming just went on and on. "Isn't that terrible?" said the woman at the table.

"Yes," said the man. "It isn't very pleasant for a picnic." At last, the man turned to

Boodles and said, "Maybe if you would give him your balloon, we'd have some peace and quiet around here."

"I'm not going to give that kid my balloon," said Boodles. "I'm going to take my balloon home. I like it." The screaming grew even louder.

"Are you a boy scout?" asked the man.

"Not yet," replied Boodles. "I'm a cub scout."

"Well, what about your good deed for the day?" the man asked.

"No way," said Boodles. "Let the kid yell!"

"You mean," said the man, "you don't want to help us by doing a good deed?"

"Well," said Boodles, "if an older person needed to go across the street, I'd help, of course. But I'm not going to give that kid my balloon."

The little boy went on screaming. The tears rolled down his cheeks.

Boodles looked around. He was the only one at their table with a balloon. Here and there at the other tables, children had balloons tied to their chairs or to their wrists. They were all very small children. Some

13

were even babies. Boodles looked at Eddie. Eddie didn't have a balloon. He didn't have any peanuts or any money left, either.

The little boy was still screaming. The red balloon was a small dot high in the sky.

The people sitting at the boy's table had their hands over their ears, trying to shut out the shrill sound. The boy's mother looked as if she might start crying herself.

Suddenly, Boodles got up with his red balloon and ran to the little boy. Everyone watched as Boodles held out the balloon. There was a sudden silence. A smile came over the child's face. "I'll just tie this balloon to your wrist and then you won't lose it again," said Boodles.

Now everyone was smiling. They all started clapping as Boodles went back to his own table. When he sat down, the man reached out and patted Boodles on the shoulder. "Good scout," he said. "I'll buy you another balloon. You've done your good deed for the day."

Boodles was really surprised. "Thanks, mister," said Boodles. "But only little kids need balloons. Do you think we could have our lunch now, Mom?"

"Oh, my," said his mother, "I almost for-
got about eating with all that screaming
going on. Here are some ham and cheese
sandwiches for you and Eddie."

15

Boodles and Eddie took them eagerly and started eating as though they had never seen food before.

"Thanks, Mrs. Carey," said Eddie between bites. "These are great!"

Boodles reached for a cookie. "I was really hungry," he said. "And you can't eat a balloon!"

·3·

Tricks to Learn

The afternoon show was about to begin. Mrs. Carey had bought tickets for Eddie and Boodles, and now they were finding their way to the seats in the big tent.

"I think those are our seats right in front," said Eddie.

As soon as they sat down, the circus band began playing and the curtains at the end of the tent opened. First, the ringmaster stepped forward and announced, "You are about to see the greatest show on earth!"

The audience began clapping. Trapeze artists, lion tamers, clowns, dogs dancing in their funny collars, elephants with riders in beautiful costumes, acrobats, and even the horses pulling the lions' cage paraded around the tent. "Hey, that dog looks a little like Poochie," shouted Boodles. "I wonder if he's going to do some tricks."

After the opening parade, the acrobats took center stage, followed by galloping horses with plumes on their heads.

And to Boodles's delight, the dog that looked like Poochie began showing off his tricks. He walked around on his hind legs, he jumped through hoops, and he played dead on command. The other dog came over to the audience and offered his paw to the children. Eddie burst out laughing when the dog came to him and held out his paw. When the dog pranced away, Eddie turned to Boodles and said, "That dog was the best part of the circus. I'd like to have a dog exactly like him."

"Oh," said Boodles, "I don't think he's so great. I think Poochie could do any of those tricks."

Eddie looked a little doubtful.

"Someday, I'll show you," Boodles insisted.

The boys watched the dogs finish their tricks. One of the dogs behaved in a manner not quite proper for the show, leaving a puddle in the sawdust. Everyone laughed and applauded. A clown went over with a bucket of sand and threw it over the puddle. This made everyone laugh even louder. "Now Poochie could do *that* trick," said Eddie.

When the dogs finished their tricks, some clowns came out in an old car. They climbed out of the car, tumbling over each other. One clown drove the car around in a circle. The car jerked and sputtered. Smoke poured out of the exhaust pipes.

"Whew," exclaimed Boodles, "that car sure smells. Those clowns need to fix it up."

"I think that smelly car is supposed to be part of their act," said Eddie.

The clowns opened the hood of the car and began using big tools to fix the engine. The smoke stopped coming out of the exhaust pipe and everyone clapped.

Boodles and Eddie joined in and laughed as the clowns started clapping, too.

"I don't see any more smoke, but I sure smell smoke," said Boodles.

"Me, too," said Eddie.

"Hey, look," shouted a man next to them, "there's a fire over there!" A small fire was crackling near the entrance. The clowns dropped their tools and started running toward the entrance.

Boodles stood up and shouted, "Hey, get those buckets of sand!" One of the clowns turned around and dashed back to pick up a bucket of sand. He ran to the fire and threw the sand on the flames, smothering the fire before it could spread farther.

"Good for you, Boodles!" Eddie exclaimed.

"Well, kid," said the man next to Boodles, "that was pretty quick thinking."

"Oh, we learn about putting out fires in our cub scout meetings," said Boodles. "You can't go camping unless you know how to put out a camp fire."

The clown who had put out the fire came over to Boodles and Eddie. "Thanks a lot for shouting to us. I was running for the fire extinguisher, but the pail of sand was much closer. How about visiting me backstage after the show?"

Boodles and Eddie looked at each other. "Great!" they both said.

The ringmaster went on announcing all the acts, and the show finished with everyone standing and cheering.

Eddie and Boodles went back to the dressing rooms and found the clowns wiping off their makeup and putting away their cos-

21

tumes. They saw the clown they had spoken to before lunch. He and his dog both gave them a funny bow. The other dog kept following the clown who had invited them backstage.

"Hi, boys. Come in and have a seat, but be careful when you sit down. Sometimes my dog, Charlie, jumps up in the chair just as you're sitting down. That's one of his favorite tricks. My name's Fred Beamer, but you can call me Turnip. I always turn up in the funniest places, so all my friends started calling me Turnip. What are your names, boys?"

Boodles laughed and said, "This is my friend Eddie Wilson, and I'm Boswell Carey, only everyone calls me Boodles."

"Boodles!" exclaimed Turnip. "Now that's a good clown name! Have you got a dog, too?"

"Yes," replied Boodles. "I have a really nice dog named Poochie, and I'd sure like to teach him some tricks like the ones your dog knows. How can I do that, Mr. Turnip?"

"Just Turnip, Boodles," said Mr. Beamer, laughing. "Tricks, huh? Well, first of all, you have to believe you can do it. You have to

love your dog, and your dog has to love you
back. Then he'll do all kinds of things for
you."

"Oh, I love Poochie, and I know he loves
me," said Boodles.

23

"I saw you giving your dog some tidbits and patting him after he did his tricks," said Eddie. "Do you always do that?"

"Oh, sure," said Turnip. "You have to let him know he's been a good dog and done the right thing. You reward him. The way you speak to him helps a lot, too."

"Wow, I'm going to go right home and teach Poochie some tricks," said Boodles excitedly. "Come on, Eddie. We've got a lot to do."

"Bye, Turnip," said Eddie. "Thanks a lot for your help."

"Good-bye, boys," said Turnip. "Boodles, if you need any more help with teaching tricks, remember we'll be back in April."

"Hey, Turnip, I just might bring Poochie to meet you after he's learned all his tricks. We could join the circus!" Boodles called back. He and Eddie started running toward the exit. "What do you think of that, Eddie?"

Eddie just stared at him and said, "Boodles, is that for real, or is that a funzie?"

·4·

Boodles Tries His Best

Boodles decided that if he was going to be a clown, he ought to look like a clown.

One Sunday afternoon, while his mother and father were out for a drive, Boodles went upstairs. He looked for some makeup in his mother's dressing table. Poochie followed him and watched with great interest while Boodles rummaged around in the drawers.

"Poochie," Boodles said, "I don't think

Mom would mind if I borrowed some of her makeup. She thinks clowns are lots of fun. I know she would want me to look just right as a famous clown." He found some lipsticks, an eyebrow pencil, a large box of powder, and something with a brush that said BLUSH—OLD ROSE.

"I'll just put some of this lipstick on my cheeks and nose," Boodles said to Poochie. He spread big red smears on his face. Next, Boodles made large black circles around his eyes and freckles on top of his nose with the eyebrow pencil.

"Now for some powder, Poochie," said Boodles. He smacked the powder puff all over his face. The clouds of powder made him sneeze. "I wonder how Mom can use this stuff, Poochie," he said between sneezes.

Last, he brushed Old Rose on his forehead and chin. Then he gazed at his reflection in the mirror. "Well, what do you think, Poochie?" asked Boodles. "Do I look like a clown now?"

Boodles turned around to give Poochie a better look. Poochie backed away and started barking. "Poochie, it's me," Boodles said. Poochie ran out the door and down the

stairs. Boodles followed him. "Hey, it's me—Boodles, your pal!"

Just as Boodles reached the bottom of the stairs, his mother opened the front door.

"What is all this noise, Boodles? Why is Poochie bark—" Then she saw Boodles. Her mouth dropped open. "Boodles, what have you been doing?" she asked. "Where did you get that makeup on your face?"

"Oh, Mom," said Boodles, "I just borrowed some things from your drawer so I could look like a real clown."

"Boodles, you know you should ask before you borrow anything," she said. "I'll get some cold cream and you can wipe off that makeup."

"But I have it exactly the way I want it," said Boodles. "I was just asking Poochie how he liked it. But I don't think he knows me now."

When he heard his name, Poochie poked his head around the doorway. He started barking at Boodles again.

"He doesn't know you with all that stuff on your face," his mother laughed. "You don't even look like something a mother would want around!" Poochie kept barking. "I don't think Poochie is very impressed."

Boodles went toward Poochie with his hand out to pat him, but Poochie backed away again. This time, he whimpered. His tail was tucked between his legs. "Come on, Poochie," said Boodles, "you know me. We've got to get started on learning some tricks. We could even put some makeup on you, Poochie." Poochie didn't like this idea at all. He ran toward the basement.

"Boodles . . ." his mother said.

"Why can't I wait until after Eddie and the other kids see how great I look?" asked Boodles. "I'll get it off after that. It'll be easy to wipe off."

"My goodness, you can't leave it on until you go to school!" Mrs. Carey exclaimed. She went into the bathroom and came back with a jar of cold cream. "The longer you leave it on, the harder it is to get off. Now rub this on your face. Then wipe everything off with these tissues."

"Couldn't I at least show Dad?" Boodles asked hopefully.

"Your father has gone to pick up Hal and his friend at the fairgrounds," his mother said. "Now get to work!"

Sadly, Boodles went into the bathroom. He put some cold cream on his face. He smeared it around until the red lipstick, the black eyebrow pencil, the white powder, and the Old Rose were all blended into a horrible mess. "Poochie ought to see me now," said Boodles. "He'd really be scared."

It was taking a lot of tissues to wipe off the makeup. "It's not all coming off, Mom," Boodles called.

"Keep using the cold cream and tissues," his mother said.

Boodles tried more cold cream and tissues. Some more makeup came off. Maybe I should try soap and water, he decided. He scrubbed his face with a soapy washcloth. He still could see red and black marks on his face. The washcloth was a mess.

His mother came in to look at him. "It looks as if that's all you're going to get off for now, Boodles," she said. "It will slowly wear off as you wash up each day. The more you rub your face, the redder you seem to get."

On Monday morning, Boodles went off to school. His face was red and blotchy. There were faint black circles around his eyes and a couple of black freckle marks still showed on top of his nose.

Boodles walked into his classroom. Eddie Wilson came over to him. "Boodles, you don't look so good," he said. "What's the matter with you?"

"I'm okay," replied Boodles. "I tried using my mother's makeup to look like a clown, but I couldn't get it all off. I rubbed and I rubbed."

"Are you sure that's what it is?" asked Eddie. "You look like you have a rash or something."

Anna Patricia Wallace cried out, "Boodles has a rash. Boodles has a rash!"

The children were gathered around Boodles when Miss Miller, their teacher, came in. She raised her eyebrows and said, "Well, what has Boodles done today?"

She walked over to the group and looked at Boodles. Then she took his hand. "Come with me, Boodles," she said. "I'm taking you to the nurse's office."

"But, Miss Miller, I can explain," said Boodles.

"No talking," Miss Miller told him. "The sooner we get you to the nurse, the better. You don't look well at all. You may have to go home. We'll see what the nurse says."

As Miss Miller opened the nurse's door, Boodles pulled back. He was afraid to go in.

Miss Miller gently pushed him into the office. "It's all right, Boodles," she said. "Mrs. Wyler is here to help you. We have to find out why your face is so red."

Mrs. Wyler put her hand on Boodles's forehead. "He doesn't seem warm at all," she said. "Open your mouth, Boodles. I want to look at your throat."

Boodles opened his mouth very wide. The nurse looked at his throat. "Your throat looks fine," she said. Then she looked closely at his face. "Boodles, have you put something on your face?"

"I guess you might say that," said Boodles. "I guess you might say I tried using some of my mother's makeup to make a clown face. Do you think I'll always look like this?"

Miss Miller and Mrs. Wyler laughed and laughed. "Oh, Boodles," said the nurse, "I don't think you will look like that forever, but it might take a few days for your face to look right. You must have rubbed it very hard!"

"Boodles," said Miss Miller, "whatever you do, you always do your best, even when it's painting your face like a clown's! Come

on, let's go back to the classroom and tell everyone you're all right."

Mrs. Wyler was still laughing. "Next time, Boodles," she said, "remember that clowns use a special greasepaint to make their clown faces. Greasepaint is a lot easier to get off."

"We'd better tell the other kids then," said Boodles, "in case somebody else gets the same idea and tries to be a clown, too."

·5·

Boodles and the Police Officers

It was Friday afternoon. Boodles and Eddie had decided to walk home from school. It was fun scuffing through the dry leaves. The trees were almost bare, and a cold wind made them button up their jackets. Suddenly, they heard sirens.

"Eddie!" shouted Boodles. "I think that siren is coming this way!"

Now they could see flashing red and blue lights way down the street.

"Oh, boy!" said Eddie. "It's a police car. Let's see where it goes!"

Whoo-ee! Whoo-ee! The white-and-blue police car whizzed right past them.

"It's headed for the school!" shouted Boodles. "Let's go back!"

The two boys raced back up the street toward the school. Huffing and puffing, they turned the last corner. There was the police cruiser parked right in the playground.

"Cars aren't allowed on the playground," gasped Eddie.

"Something bad must be happening," said Boodles.

Running closer, they saw several grown-ups and a group of girls from their class clustered around Mr. Bowen, the school janitor, who was kneeling on the ground.

The boys hurried across the street. Now two police officers had gotten out of the cruiser and were making people move back. Eddie and Boodles peeked between the grown-ups.

"Oh, no!" said Boodles. "It's Annie Pat, and she isn't moving." Eddie looked. Sure enough, he knew Anna Patricia's red jacket and her red tassle cap. She was lying on her back, and her eyes were closed.

36

"What's wrong with Annie Pat?" Boodles asked one of the people standing by.

"She fell off the jungle gym," answered the girl next to him. "I hope she didn't break anything."

Boodles and Eddie looked at each other. Poor Anna Patricia!

The taller of the police officers was carrying a box marked FIRST AID, which he placed on the ground.

"The school nurse has already gone home," Mr. Bowen was telling him. "That's why I called you."

"Does anyone here know this girl's telephone number?" asked the other police officer.

"I do," said the girl who was standing next to Boodles.

"Come with me," the officer told her as he walked back toward the cruiser. "The dispatcher at the police station can call her parents and tell them to meet us at the hospital."

Suddenly Anna Patricia blinked. She stared up at the tall police officer. "Oh, oh," she said weakly. "What happened?"

"You had a bad fall," he said in a gentle voice. "I think it just knocked the wind out

of you, but we're going to take you to the
hospital to make sure." He asked Anna Patricia to move first one arm and then the
other. She wiggled her hands and her feet.
Then she lifted each leg.

"Everything seems to be working," said
the police officer who had called the station.
"Can you sit up?"

Slowly, Anna Patricia sat up. She looked around at all the people. "I guess I'm okay now," she said. "Thank you." Carefully, she stood up, supported by Mr. Bowen and the tall police officer. "I'm Officer Tom Rossi," he told her, "and this is Officer Fred Morris. You still look a bit wobbly. Let's get you into the cruiser."

Anna Patricia's eyes opened wide. "Do you mean I'll get to ride in the police car with sirens blowing?"

Officer Rossi laughed. "Well, not with the siren going. We use that only in emergencies. But we'll put on the flashers so that everybody will know we're on an important job."

Now that people saw that Anna Patricia was all right, they turned away and went about their business. Officer Morris leaned down to pick up the first-aid box. Boodles tugged on his arm.

"Excuse me, Officer," he said, "but I thought the police just chased bad guys and put them in jail."

"Oh, no," said Officer Morris. "Our main job is to help people. Sometimes we have to catch bad people so the town will be safe.

But the best part of our job is helping. If you are ever lost, call us and we'll get you home. And we help keep the traffic untangled so that accidents won't happen. We keep an eye on your street at night to be sure everything is okay. And sometimes, we take young ladies to the hospital."

"I remember," said Eddie. "You helped at the circus parade. You kept people out of the way and led the band down the street."

Boodles watched Officer Rossi help Anna Patricia into the patrol car. "I wish I could ride in the police car," he said. "I wish I could sound the siren and flash the lights."

Officer Morris chuckled. "Not today," he said, "but maybe someday. Did you know we are coming to your school next week?"

Boodles and Eddie were surprised. "Why are you coming to school? Does somebody else need help?" Boodles asked.

Officer Morris smiled. "Maybe you do."

Boodles stepped back. "What do you mean?" he asked.

"Well," he said, "we're coming to give a bicycle-safety demonstration. Do you have a bicycle?"

"Sure," said Boodles and Eddie together.

"We'll be seeing you on Tuesday, then,"

said the officer, and he waved good-bye as he hurried off to the waiting patrol car.

On Monday, Boodles could hardly wait to get his winter jacket buttoned and rush off to school. He was still pulling on his gloves when he met Eddie at the school-bus stop.

"We know something nobody else knows," he reminded Eddie.

On the bus, they met Joe and Sidney. Sidney, who was one of the boys' best friends, had an interesting name for a girl. "We know something you don't know," said Eddie.

"Tell us," said the children.

"No," said Boodles. "You'll find out in school. But it's about the police."

"The police!" Joe and Sidney looked at each other.

"Don't worry," said Boodles. "It's something nice about the police."

Sure enough, as soon as they were settled in their seats at school, the teacher made an announcement. "Tomorrow," she said, "we are going to have a very special program. The police are coming to put on a bicycle-safety show. If you have a bicycle, be sure to ride it to school if you can. I hope those boys and girls who live nearby will share their bikes with the students who come on the bus."

"We know the police officers," said Eddie, feeling very important.

"Their names are Officer Rossi and Officer Morris," added Boodles.

The whole class was excited and everyone talked at once, wanting to know how Eddie and Boodles knew about the police. Finally, Miss Miller got them to quiet down. A few of the children hadn't heard about Annie Pat, so she told them how she rode in a police car to the hospital. They were very impressed.

"Luckily, Anna Patricia wasn't seriously hurt," said Miss Miller. "The rest of us will meet Officers Morris and Rossi tomorrow."

Everyone was still excited the next morning. Bicycles seemed to be rolling down every street. It was fun not to take the bus for a change. When Boodles and Eddie had stopped at the last corner to watch for cars, Eddie happened to look back.

"Boodles! Boodles! Look who's coming!" called Eddie.

Boodles looked back. There, racing up the street with his ears flopping, was Poochie.

He caught up to Boodles and jumped all over him for joy.

"Oh, Poochie," said Boodles. "What should I do with you? I can't take you back or I'll be late. Here." He scooped up the wiggly dog with both arms and plopped him in the saddle basket of his bicycle. "Maybe," added Boodles, "you can stay in the principal's office till it's time to go home."

But the school rule was, *No dogs inside.* So Boodles had to leave Poochie on the front step, looking very sad. "Wait right there for me, Poochie!" said Boodles. "Maybe I can get permission to take you home at lunch." Poochie sat and drooped.

Boodles could hardly keep his mind on his class work. The hours before recess seemed so long. At last, the bell rang. Everyone raced out to the school yard, and there was Poochie, right at Boodles's heels.

What a surprise they found on the playground! White chalk roadways covered the whole place. Road signs stood here and there, at corners and crossings. Even a pretend railroad crossing was marked. Officers Morris and Rossi were waiting on one side of the course.

Soon, all the bikers were lined up. One at

a time, they rode carefully around the course. "Always keep to the right," said Officer Rossi. He stood at the pretend crossroad and blew his whistle for start and stop. "Follow the same rules as automobiles," warned Officer Morris from the sideline. He was writing each child's name and score in a notebook.

Now it was Boodles's turn. He and Poochie had been waiting quietly, watching each rider. Boodles got on his bike and started around the course.

Boodles rode his bike very carefully. He stayed on the right. He obeyed every sign. When he passed Eddie, his friend gave a victory sign. But then Boodles heard chuckles. Everybody was laughing. Why are they laughing? worried Boodles. I'm sure I'm driving the right way.

Then he went around a sharp curve and started back. Right behind him came Poochie. The little dog pranced around the bend and trotted along right behind the bike. When the bike stopped, Poochie sat down. When the bike sped up, Poochie sped up. People laughed and laughed. At least they're not laughing at me, thought Boodles.

After everyone had had a turn, Officer
Rossi stepped forward. He gave a special
bike license, a bike-safety book, and a blue
ribbon to each rider. At last, he came up to

Poochie. Boodles thought he was going to scold the little dog.

"What is his name?" asked Officer Rossi.

"Poochie," answered Boodles. "I shouldn't have let him follow me this morning."

"Poochie is the best follower I ever saw," said Officer Rossi. He leaned down and pinned a blue ribbon on Poochie's collar. Then he handed Boodles a special card for Poochie. "Your dog is a real clown," he said. "Anybody who can make people laugh the way Poochie did should be in the circus."

Boodles laughed happily. "Oh, we're both going to be in the circus someday," said Boodles.

·6·

Fun in the Snow

That Friday night, Eddie slept over at the Careys' house. When the boys woke up on Saturday morning, they looked out on a pure white world. It had snowed all during the night. Everything was covered with snow. The rooftops were piled high with it, and snow hung on all the trees.

Eddie and Boodles thought the snow was wonderful. They could hardly wait to get out and play. Neither could Poochie. He loved snow, too. It was so deep that Eddie and

Boodles could hardly walk through it. Poochie couldn't walk in the snow at all. He had
to jump through it.

"Poochie looks like a rabbit." Boodles
laughed as he watched the little dog bounce
along. They made their way to the hill in
front of Eddie's house. It was already covered with boys and girls belly flopping on
their sleds.

Boodles flopped down into the fresh snow.
Lying on his back, he moved his arms up
and down. His arms pushed the snow into
little piles. He got up carefully and looked
behind him. Pointing, he said to Eddie,
"Look, I made an angel!"

"An angel!" said Eddie. "Looks more like
a helicopter to me." He looked closely at it
again. "Yes, it's definitely a whirlybird.
Let's see if I can make one, too."

Eddie flopped back in the snow and
moved his arms up and down just the way
Boodles had done. When he got up, Boodles
said, "We've got to make these look more
like helicopters. I'll just slide my boots along
the bottom here and we'll have the helicopter runners." Boodles shuffled along at the
bottom of their snow pictures, making
marks that looked like runners.

Eddie studied the results. "Now they look more like big flowers growing out of the ground," he said.

Boodles laughed. "Okay, you try again. See if you can make another helicopter."

While Eddie kept trying to make helicopters, Boodles was busy rolling a big ball of snow.

"What are you making now, Boodles?" asked Eddie.

"I'm going to make a snowman!" said Boodles. "I've got enough snow for his big stomach."

The boys rolled two more balls, one for his chest and one for his head. When they had piled the balls on top of each other, Eddie said, "Your snowman doesn't have a face."

Boodles found some sticks that looked just the right shape for the snowman's nose and mouth. But he couldn't find anything for eyes. "I could use some stones, but they're all covered up by the snow," he said.

"Wait a minute!" cried Eddie. "I know! Mom has some radishes in the refrigerator. They'd make nice bright eyes!"

Eddie ran into the house and came out with two big radishes. He stuck them into

49

the snowman's face. Now the snowman had eyes.

"He looks like he's been crying," said Boodles. "He's been rubbing his eyes!"

Suddenly, Boodles looked around. "Where's Poochie?" he asked. Both boys looked and looked. At last, they spotted snow flying under the big pine tree. They ran over. There was Poochie, digging and digging. Finally, he came to something blue. He tugged and pulled it out of the snow.

"Why, that's my scarf! I must have left it outside yesterday," said Boodles. "Oh, Poochie, aren't you smart! This is just the thing for our snowman."

The boys ran over and tied the blue scarf around the snowman. It hardly went around his fat snow neck, but it looked great.

"Now you won't get cold," said Eddie to the snowman. Boodles laughed and laughed.

All this fun in the snow had loosened Eddie's jacket zipper. Snow had gotten inside. The snow had melted, and now Eddie was feeling pretty wet. "I feel like a melted snowball, Boodles," he said. "Let's go inside."

They headed for the Wilsons' house. In-

side, they took off their wet jackets and put
their boots by the door. There was a fire
burning in the fireplace.

"Oh, boy," said Eddie. "Listen to that fire
crackle!"

Eddie dropped down into a chair near the fireplace. He said to Boodles, "This is great! You better cozy up!"

"Cozy up is right," said Boodles. He stretched out on the floor, his head snuggled against a cushion.

"It feels good to be warm," said Eddie. He slipped from the chair to the floor and fell sound asleep.

Even Boodles was too tired and cold for more winter fun. Soon both boys were asleep on the living-room floor in front of the fireplace.

Eddie's mother came into the living room. Well, she said to herself, they seem to be taking a long winter's nap. She checked the fire screen to make sure no sparks could fly out and began to tiptoe away. There was a scratching sound at the front door. She opened the door. It was Poochie! "Come in, Poochie," said Mrs. Wilson. "I'll bet you need to get warm, too."

Poochie ran into the living room. His tail started wagging when he saw Boodles. He licked Boodles's face. Boodles was so sleepy, he didn't even open his eyes. "Beat it, Eddie," he said very slowly. "Stop bothering

me. Go make a helicopter in the snow."

Poochie lay down next to Boodles. He put his head on Boodles's arm and soon he was asleep, too. Only the snowman stayed awake.

·7·

Poochie's Tricks

Spring had come. The days were getting warmer, and the children were beginning to talk about what they were going to do in the summer.

One day Boodles and Eddie saw posters about the circus coming back to town. Boodles was excited. He had almost forgotten about becoming a clown. Now he would be able to talk to Turnip again. If he and Poochie really worked on their tricks, maybe

Turnip would ask them to join the circus.

Boodles was sure that Poochie was just as smart as Turnip's dog, Charlie.

That very day, Boodles said, "Poochie, I'm going to teach you some tricks."

First, Boodles held up Poochie's front legs so that the dog stood up on his hind legs. Once Poochie seemed used to the idea, they took a little break. Then Boodles stood Poochie up again. Boodles held a dog biscuit way above Poochie's head. When Boodles let go of Poochie's paws, Poochie stood alone for a minute. "Good dog, Poochie!" Boodles told him. "Poochie, you're going to be a circus dog yet!"

Poochie wagged his tail. He seemed to know that Boodles was trying to get him to do something. Perhaps he was just not sure what it was.

The next day, after school, Boodles stood Poochie on his hind legs again, saying, "Poochie, just think of all the dog biscuits you're getting!" Poochie seemed to agree that the dog biscuits were very good. He put his right paw on Boodles's leg and barked for more.

A week went by. Finally, when Boodles had given Poochie a whole box of dog biscuits, Poochie could hobble on his back legs alone for a few moments.

Boodles was delighted. He patted his dog and said, "You're a circus dog all right! Let's go show Anna Patricia what you can do. You're just as good as any dog in the circus."

Boodles got the leash, and soon they were on their way to Annie Pat's house.

When Boodles rang the front doorbell, Anna Patricia's mother opened the door. "Hello, Boodles," she said. "If you want to see Annie Pat, she's in the backyard."

"Thanks," replied Boodles. He and Poochie ran around the house to the backyard. "Annie Pat," he called, "we're here to show you Poochie, the show-stopping circus performer!"

Anna Patricia laughed and said, "Boodles, do you really know how to train a dog for the circus?"

"Wait and see," said Boodles.

But when Boodles snapped his fingers for Poochie to walk on his hind legs, Poochie just sat there. Boodles held up a dog biscuit, but Poochie wouldn't move. His tongue was hanging out, and he looked a little sad. Poochie was refusing to be a circus dog.

"He looks a little chubby to me," said

Anna Patricia. "Maybe he's had too many dog biscuits. Maybe he doesn't want to be a circus dog."

"Sure he does," said Boodles. "He'll be a good circus dog. And we'll both make a lot of money."

"Well, maybe, Boodles," said Anna Patricia. "But don't count on it any time soon."

"Well, he just doesn't like walking on his hind legs all the time," said Boodles. "I'll teach him another trick he'll like better."

There was a hoop leaning against Anna Patricia's back steps. Anna Patricia picked it up and rolled it across the yard. Suddenly, Poochie jumped up and ran after her. He tried to pull the hoop away.

"The hoop!" Boodles cried. "Maybe Poochie would like to jump through the hoop!"

"It looks as if Poochie would rather bite it," Anna Patricia said.

"That means he likes it," said Boodles. "Can I borrow that hoop, Annie Pat? I want to teach Poochie to jump through it. Let's go back to my house and see if Poochie will jump through the hoop."

When they got back to Boodles's house, they went right to the backyard. Poochie liked that hoop. He liked to chase it.

"No, Poochie, that isn't right," said Anna
Patricia. "You must jump through it."

"He needs dog biscuits," said Boodles. He
ran inside and came back with a whole box
of biscuits. "Now, Annie Pat, you hold the
hoop, and I'll hold a dog biscuit."

Anna Patricia picked up the hoop and held

it up in front of Poochie. Poochie ran over and bit the hoop.

"No, Poochie," said Boodles. "You jump through the hoop. See?" Boodles held out a dog biscuit while Anna Patricia held up the hoop. But Poochie did not bother to jump. Instead, he ran around the hoop and snatched the biscuit. Then he took the hoop in his teeth and tried to pull it away from Anna Patricia.

"No, Poochie!" cried Boodles. "Like this!" Boodles jumped through the hoop. "See, Poochie?" Boodles jumped through the hoop again. "Like this!" Boodles jumped through a third time. He hoped Poochie would catch on and jump through the hoop, too.

The fourth time, Poochie jumped through the hoop right after Boodles. Boodles and Anna Patricia clapped and clapped. "Yay, Poochie!" Boodles shouted.

"I think you're right, Boodles," said Anna Patricia. "With a little more training, Poochie could be a circus dog."

When Poochie heard that, he ran over and bit the hoop again!

·8·

Poochie, the Disappearing Dog

One afternoon Boodles was outside waiting for his mother to take him to the shoe store when a truck pulled up outside his house. A man climbed out. Poochie ran to the man and jumped up, wagging his tail. The man patted Poochie on the head and said, "This is a fine dog. He has a fine pedigree. It shows all over him." He winked at Boodles.

"Yes," said Boodles's mother as she came down the front steps. "We haven't decided what kind of dog he is. What could he be?"

"Oh, I think he's some kind of beagle," said the man.

"Yes," said Boodles. "He's a thorough-bred all right. It shows all over him."

"He's a fine dog," said the man, patting Poochie on the head again.

Poochie wagged his tail again. He seemed pleased at all these compliments.

"Come along," said Mrs. Carey to Boodles. "I need to get home in time to start dinner."

"I'll see you again," said the man. "Say, do you want your driveway repaved? I'm just finishing up at the Larkins' house the next block over. They'll vouch for my work."

"No," said Boodles's mother, "we don't need anything like that now. Thank you, anyway."

"Well, take my card," the man said. "I'll be happy to give you an estimate anytime." He tipped his hat, got into the truck, and drove off.

"He's a nice man, Mom," Boodles said.

"He seemed to be," Mrs. Carey agreed. "It's too bad we don't have any work for him." She looked at her watch. "You'd better put Poochie in the house."

When Boodles got back from the store, he let Poochie out into the backyard. "Poochie," said Boodles, "you can have some fun while I eat dinner. Then we can try more circus tricks. The dog biscuits are disappearing fast, Poochie, so you're going to have to shape up pretty soon." Poochie yawned and stretched, then trotted off.

After the family had eaten, Boodles went out to call Poochie for his dinner. He did not come when Boodles called his name. "That's funny," said Boodles. "Poochie was here just a minute ago. You don't suppose that man took him, do you, Mom?"

"Now, Boodles," said his mother, "don't get worried. You haven't really looked for him very much. Go back outside and call him again. Maybe he's digging a hole in back of the garage. You know how he likes to bury things."

Boodles went back outside. "Poochie, Poochie, where are you?" he called. Boodles looked behind the garage. He looked in every corner of the yard, under every bush, but no Poochie. He checked the front gate to see whether it was latched. The gate was slightly loose.

Boodles ran inside the house. "Mom, Dad, I think Poochie got out through the front gate 'cause it's not latched. Do you think he'll find his way home?"

"Oh, I'm sure he'll find his way home," replied his father, "but if someone took him, then we should call the police or perhaps the dog pound. Why don't we wait awhile longer and see if he comes back by himself."

Boodles went back outside and started down the street, calling, "Poochie, come home." He asked several of the neighbors whether they had seen his dog, but they all just shook their heads. Mr. Farnsworth, at the end of the block, said he would call Boodles on the telephone if he saw Poochie.

Boodles walked home slowly. Poochie, you've just got to come back, he said to himself.

Boodles went in the kitchen to talk to his mother. Mrs. Carey was cleaning up the dinner dishes. "Mom, what can I do about Poochie?"

"Boodles," she said, "you'll just have to be patient. Let's see if he finds his way home. Let's wait awhile before we call anyone about him."

63

"Mom, maybe he left 'cause he didn't like
me teaching him tricks. Do you suppose he
got tired of me trying to make him walk on
his hind legs? Maybe he didn't want all
those dog biscuits."

"We'll wait twenty more minutes," his mother said. "Maybe Poochie wanted a chance to run on his own. Maybe he was a little tired of all this trick teaching. I feel sure he'll be back. Why don't you go over to Eddie's house? Poochie might have gone over there. You go over to Eddie's so often, Poochie probably knows the way alone."

Boodles decided to call Eddie on the telephone first. He was about to pick up the receiver when he heard a knock at the front door. Boodles opened the door. There was the man who wanted to repave their driveway. He was holding Poochie in his arms.

"Say, sonny," said the man, "your dog was all the way down the next block visiting me while I was working at the Larkins'. I thought you might be wondering where he was. He's a pretty friendly dog. You better keep an eye on him."

Poochie wiggled out of the man's arms and jumped on Boodles. "Hey, Poochie." Boodles laughed. "Here I've been trying to teach you circus tricks and you already have a trick—a disappearing trick!"

"Now you see him, now you don't!" the man said, and then he chuckled.

·9·

Poochie,
the Trick Dog

The circus would be in town in barely a week. Boodles decided to try to teach Poochie one more trick.

"Here, Poochie!" he called. But Poochie wouldn't come. "Here, Poochie—a dog biscuit!" said Boodles.

Poochie wasn't interested. Boodles was worried. Poochie loved dog biscuits. If Poochie wouldn't eat a dog biscuit, he must be sick.

Poochie looked very sad. Suddenly, he threw up. Now Boodles was really worried.

"Mom," said Boodles, "Poochie is sick. We better get him to the vet right away. Can you drive us to the animal hospital?"

When Boodles and his mother and Poochie arrived at the animal hospital, Poochie was glad to see the veterinarian. Dr. Fellows was a good friend. Poochie licked his hand.

"I think Poochie likes to come here," Boodles said. "It makes him feel important."

Then Boodles told Dr. Fellows about trying to teach Poochie tricks. "But he won't even eat a dog biscuit now," Boodles said.

Dr. Fellows examined Poochie. He weighed him on a special scale. "This dog has gained two pounds!" he exclaimed. "But dog biscuits alone shouldn't have made him sick. What else have you been feeding him?"

"Just his dog food," Boodles responded. He knew he shouldn't give Poochie human food.

Then Dr. Fellows asked, "Could Poochie have eaten something you didn't give him? Something rich, for instance?"

"I wonder if Mrs. Squires might have

given Poochie a snack," said Boodles's
mother. "He sometimes goes next door to
visit her. We'll have to ask her."

The veterinarian said, "Well, he should be
all right in the morning, but you'd better
leave him overnight with me."

Poochie wagged his tail.

"This dog is the friendliest dog I have ever known," said Dr. Fellows. "He makes friends with every boarder we have in the kennel. All right, young man," he said to Boodles. "Poochie will see you tomorrow."

"Good-bye, Poochie!" said Boodles. "See you soon!"

When Poochie saw Boodles and his mother leaving, he began to whimper and tug on his leash. Poochie wouldn't be quiet. He wanted to go with them.

Boodles patted him on the head. He said, "Don't be afraid, Poochie. You'll be away for one night. I'll be back to pick you up tomorrow."

When Boodles got home, the first thing he did was to go next door to see Mrs. Squires.

When she answered the door, Boodles said, "Hi, Mrs. Squires. When my dog, Poochie, visits you, do you ever feed him?"

"Why, as a matter of fact, I do, Boodles," she answered. "Is that a problem? Just yesterday, I had some leftover lasagne, and he seemed to enjoy it."

"Lasagne!" said Boodles. "Poochie isn't used to human food, Mrs. Squires. I'm afraid it might have made him sick."

"Oh, dear," said Mrs. Squires. "I would never want to hurt Poochie."

"It's okay," said Boodles. "Poochie had to go to the vet, but he'll be home tomorrow. Next time, Mrs. Squires, could you please not feed Poochie—even if he begs?"

"Oh, I won't," she said. "I'll just give him a pat instead."

The next day was Saturday. Boodles's mother and father were busy in the morning. They couldn't take Boodles to pick up Poochie. Boodles decided to call Eddie.

He quickly dialed Eddie's number. "Hello, Eddie! Can you help me rescue my dog?" said Boodles jokingly.

Eddie's father agreed to drive Boodles and Eddie to the animal hospital. When they arrived, Mr. Wilson and Eddie waited in the car while Boodles went into the veterinarian's office. He sat in the waiting room while Dr. Fellows went to get Poochie.

In a few minutes, Dr. Fellows came through the door with Poochie on his leash. Poochie had already spied Boodles. He pounced and pulled, dragging the doctor across the floor.

Suddenly, he was free. Nobody ever saw

such an excited dog. He was so excited that he jumped and jumped. Finally, he jumped so hard that he flipped all the way over backward and landed on his feet again.

Boodles could hardly believe it. He hugged the wiggling dog.

"Oh, Poochie," he said, "That is the best trick I ever saw. I love you and I think you are wonderful."

Poochie must have thought he was wonderful, too, because when Boodles stood up, he jumped and jumped and yipped and yipped, and all at once he flipped over again.

Boodles couldn't get over it. He hugged Poochie again and told him over and over how wonderful he was.

The veterinarian watched them. "You know," he said, "love works even better than dog biscuits."

"You mean," said Boodles, "that I can help him learn tricks with hugs and happy words?"

"Yes, indeed," said the vet. "Just try it. Then maybe Poochie will get back to his normal weight!"

Boodles took Poochie's leash and, together, they pranced out of the office.

"Thank you! Thank you, Doctor!" Boodles called back as Poochie pulled him toward the car.

Eddie leaned out the car window. "Hurrah!" he called. "Poochie looks all better now." He opened the car door and Poochie jumped in. First he licked Eddie's face, then he licked Boodles's face.

"I think this dog is glad to be with you two boys again," said Mr. Wilson. "He must really love you."

"Guess what, Mr. Wilson," said Boodles excitedly. "He loves us so much, he taught himself a new trick."

"This I have to see," said Mr. Wilson.

"Wait till we get home," promised Boodles.

When the car pulled up to the Careys' front door, Boodles unclipped Poochie's leash. Poochie was the first to jump out of the car. Mrs. Carey was waiting for them in the front yard. The little dog bounced down the walk and then he saw Boodles's mother. With a glad bark he raced to Mrs. Carey, and suddenly he flipped all the way over backward again.

"Wow!" called Eddie. "What a trick!"

Eddie and his father clapped and clapped.
So Poochie flipped again. Boodles leaned
down and hugged and hugged him and told
him how great he was.

"Now how did Poochie learn that trick?"
asked Mrs. Carey. "Did Dr. Fellows teach it
to him?"

"No," said Boodles, "he taught it to himself. He taught me something, too. He taught me that love works better than dog biscuits. I guess that's what Turnip meant when he asked if I loved Poochie and if Poochie loved me. When we see him next week, I'm going to ask him whether he uses dog biscuits or love."

"I expect he uses both," said Boodles's mother. And she gave Boodles and Poochie each a big hug, one in each arm.